Fred Rogers has said that when he was a child, if he ever came across a car accident or some other terrifying scene, his mother would tell him, *"Look for the helpers."*

The Moon Came Down on Milk Street

written and illustrated by

Jean Gralley

Henry Holt and Company
New York

The moon
came down
on Milk Street,

came down with a very soft sound.

in pieces on the ground.

Who will make it right again

and set it in the air?

We will,
said the
Fire Chief.

We will,
said the Rescue Workers.

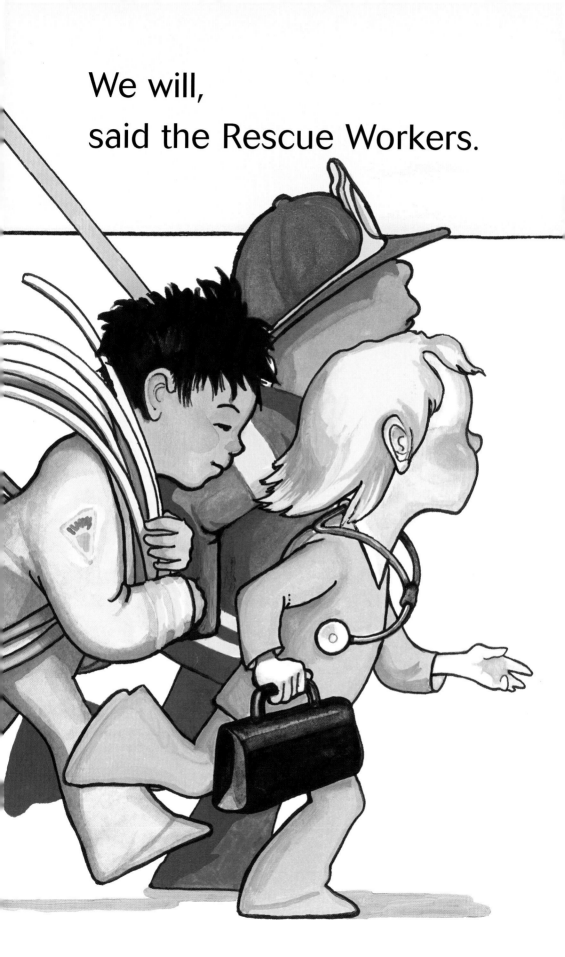

We will,
said the Helper Dogs
with short, soft hair.

We will,

said people everywhere.

Good night
to the Rescue Workers,

to the dogs

with short, soft hair.

Good night,
good night
to the Fire Chief.

Good night

to Helpers everywhere.

For Tony

Henry Holt and Company, LLC
Publishers since 1866
115 West 18th Street
New York, New York 10011
www.henryholt.com

Henry Holt is a registered trademark of Henry Holt and Company, LLC
Copyright © 2004 by Jean Gralley
All rights reserved.
Distributed in Canada by H. B. Fenn and Company Ltd.

Library of Congress Catalog Card Number: 2003023014
Full Library of Congress Cataloging-in-Publication Data available at http://catalog.loc.gov/

ISBN 0-8050-7266-7 / EAN 978-0-8050-7266-2 / First Edition—2004
The artist used gouache and mixed media on Arches paper to create the illustrations for this book.
Printed in the United States of America on acid-free paper. ∞

1 3 5 7 9 10 8 6 4 2